This book belongs

....

W9-CTF-415

This is the story of Samaritan Sam,

Can you read it? Yes, you can!

There's something else. Can you guess what?

On every page there's a mouse to spot.

Text copyright © 2006 Nick and Claire Page

This edition copyright © 2006 make believe ideas ltd.

Published by Integrity Publishers, 660 Baker's Bridge Ave., Suite 200, Franklin, TN 37067.

www.integritypublishers.com

HELPING PEOPLE WORLDWIDE EXPERIENCE *the* MANIFEST PRESENCE *of* GOD.

Manufactured in China.

The Good Samaritan

Nick and Claire Page

Illustrations by Nikky Loy

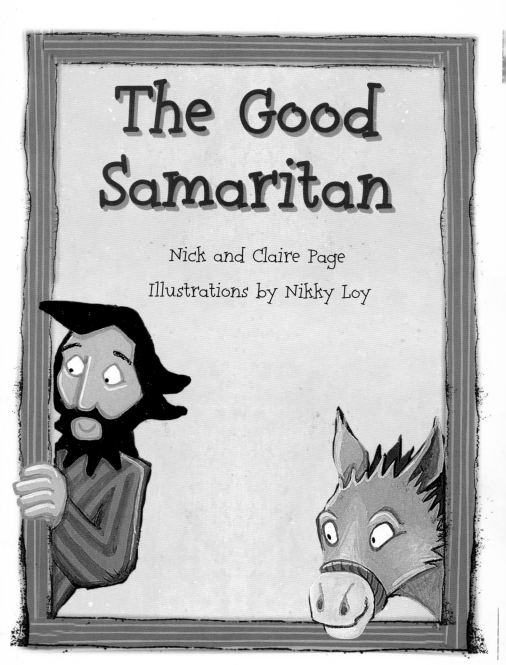

INTEGRITY
PUBLISHERS

family

Nashville

So here's the tale as I heard it.
There's this man, see?
Never done anyone any harm,
always minds his own business.
He's Izzy the Israelite. Is he? Right!
And he needs to get to Jericho, right?
And he lives in Jerusalem, see?

Well, it's a risky old road, that.
From Jerusalem to Jericho.
It's as rough as a rocky riverbed,
as winding as a wiggly worm,
as slippery as a slithery snake.

So anyway, he's walking along, is Izzy,
whistling to stop himself from being afraid.

Time goes by.
One o'clock: he's OK.
Two o'clock: on his way.
Three o'clock: it's a nice day –
blue skies above, sun shining down,
and only the rocks for shade.

Suddenly Izzy the Israelite notices
a flicker in the shadows.
Izzy's not alone. Is he? No.
There are thieves in the thickets,
robbers in the rocks,
bandits behind the boulders.

Robbers rush at him.
BIP! BAP! BOUF!
Thieves thump him.
OW! OUCH! OOF!
Bandits bash him and beat him up badly.
They take all his money, dump him in
a ditch and run away.

He's dizzy, is Izzy.
Is he? Very.
Perhaps someone will
walk by and help him.

Time goes by.
Four o'clock: no one near.
Five o'clock: sheds a tear.
Six o'clock: someone's here!

Here comes Parish the priest.

"He's holy! He'll help," says Izzy to himself.
Parish the priest sees Izzy lying by the side
of the road. And he crosses over to the other
side and keeps on walking!

**I ask you! Is that properly priestly?
Is that godly and good? No.**

Time goes by.
Seven o'clock: still no news.
Eight o'clock: badly bruised.
Nine o'clock: the sound of shoes.

Here comes Harris the temple worker.
"He's holy! He'll help," says Izzy to himself.
Harris the helper sees Izzy lying by the
side of the road. And he crosses over to
the other side and keeps on walking!
I ask you! Is that helpfully holy?
Is that godly and good? No.

Time goes by.
Ten o'clock: no light.
Eleven o'clock: what a fright!
Twelve o'clock: midnight.
Then along the road comes
Sam the Samaritan.
"He's horrible. He won't help,"
says Izzy to himself.

Now, as you know, Samaritans and Israelites,
they don't get along.
They fight like cats and dogs,
like lions and bears,
like... Israelites and Samaritans.
They're always arguing and forever fighting.

Would someone from Samaria
help someone from Israel?
What would you say?
Would someone from Israel
help someone from Samaria?
No way.

But when Sam the Samaritan sees
Izzy the Israelite lying by the side
of the road, he stops.
He steps over.
He stoops down to have a closer look.

Then Sam the Samaritan picks Izzy up and
washes out his wounds,
bandages his bruises,
cleans up his cuts.

21

Then he takes Izzy to a nearby inn
where he nurses him through the night
to the new day.
I ask you! Is that helpfully holy?
Is that godly and good? Yes!

And the next morning, Sam, he says to the innkeeper, "Here is some money to look after Izzy. If he needs anything more, give him the goods, add it to my bill, I'll repay you when I return." Then he goes on his way.

RECEPTION

And that's the tale as I heard it.
Now I ask you this.
Who showed lots of love?
Who scored the highest in holiness?
Who was godly and good?
Not Parish the priest;
Not Harris the temple helper;
But Sam, the very, very
good Samaritan.

Ready to tell

Oh no! Some of the pictures from this story have been mixed up! Can you retell the story and point to each picture in the correct order?

Picture dictionary

Encourage your child to read these harder
words from the story and gradually
develop their basic vocabulary.

bandage

boulders

donkey

money

road

robbers

rocks

thicket

walking